Chapters of Love

LOVE STORIES WITH THE LORD

RAYMOND B. BALAOD PSDP

OB

Published by:

 **OMNIBOOK**Co.

OMNIBOOK CO.
99 Wall Street, Suite 118
New York, NY 10005
USA
+1-866-216-9965
www.omnibookcompany.com

For e-book purchase: Kindle on Amazon, Barnes and Noble
Book purchase: Amazon.com, Barnes & Noble, and
www.omnibookcompany.com

Omnibook titles may be purchased in bulk for educational, business,
fund-raising, or sales promotional use. For more information
please e-mail info@omnibookcompany.com

Contents

Preface

The first volume of my short story collection entitled *"The Chapters of Life"* has introduced the three chapters of life: the past, the present, and the future. The tales in this book are meant for all who are struggling, experiencing joys and victories, and discovering new learnings in life in which God has been present in all the chapters of our lives who has made our journey challenging and meaningful.

The second volume of my collection entitled *"Chapters of Joy: Stories of finding Gladness in the Lord"* mirrors the experiences of encountering the infinite love of God despite the sufferings we have experienced in our lives. This simply reminds us that our God is a powerful God and that He is far bigger than our problems and pains. Indeed, there really is gladness with Christ amidst the world that complicates our lives and makes us hopeless. In other words, there is life in a lifeless situation when Jesus Christ will become the center of our lives.

Now, the third volume collection entitled *"Chapters of Love: Love Stories with the Lord"* focus on the love of God for us. He first loves us. And by loving us, He also teaches us how to love Him by loving our brethren, ourselves, and the whole created realities. What sustains us in all the chapters of our lives is God's love for us. Let us always open ourselves to this perfect, superabundant, and unconditional love of God so that we may grow in love and faith in the Lord.

Raymond B. Balaod, PSDP

1

Donation Box

*"For during a severe ordeal of affliction, their abundant joy and their
extreme poverty have overflowed in a wealth of generosity on their part."*
2 Cor 8:2

Mila Cervantes, who is a street vendor, has a habit of dropping coins in the donation box of Santa Maria Foundation after her long day of selling cigarettes, candy, and junk foods on the street. The donation box was located at the entrance of the foundation. She just lived a few blocks away from the SMF. She lived alone in her simple house. She did not have her own family. But she has one dog and two cats which she considered as her family.

She became the small-time benefactor of the foundation for thirty years that had corresponded to the timeline of her career as a vendor. Unfortunately, she became old and sickly. Until one day, her neighbor saw her lying on the floor inside her house unconscious. They rushed her to the nearby hospital. The doctor found out that she had a cardiac arrest. Because of her neighbor's concern, she was saved. However, the doctor told her that she must be operated on as soon as possible because there were internal complications.

"I can't! Doc. I don't have money for the operation. Just give me medicine and let me go home," Mila refused.

"I insist that you will be operated on soon," Doctor Allan demanded. "Your health is our top priority. Let us see what we can do about the expenses after the operation. We have a department here in the hospital which focuses on the financial issues of the patients. We can ask help from them."

Mila remained silent, pondering the words of Doctor Allan. A few minutes later, she finally uttered, "Are you sure you can make me well?"

Doc Allan smiled, "Yes! I can with the help of God."

"Then let's do it!"

After long hours of necessary preparation, the operation was carried on. It took six hours to finish. Fortunately, though, it was successful. She was already in the recovery room. She stayed there for two weeks. Then later she was transferred to the beautiful house of the aged adjacent to the hospital. She had her own caregiver who would make sure that she would be taken care of well.

When she was in the house for the aged, she kept on asking her private caregiver, Anna Piatro, "Where is the doctor who operated on me? I just want to thank him for what he did."

"He is always busy," Anna said. "He is the director of Don Mariano Hospital. But don't worry he will surely visit you here one of these days."

After hearing from Anna that Doc. Allan will visit her soon, she just smiled and her eyes were directed towards outside the window where the beautiful garden bloomed.

Three days later, Doc. Allan finally visited and greeted her, "Good day, ma'am! How are you feeling now?"

A little surprised and happy seeing the man who saved her life, she expressed, "I'm feeling well, Doc Allan. Thank you so much for saving my life."

"No worries," he replied.

"By the way, Doc, why is it that no one gives me my medical bills? I need that so that I could start thinking where to go to ask for some help."

Doc Allan smiled at her and looked at her eyes directly and said, "By the way, they are Doctors Vince and Michael, my colleagues here and they are also members of the Board of Directors in Don Mariano Hospital."

Then Doctors Vince and Michael had extended their hands towards Mila to shake hands.

"Your frequent donations have paid all your medical expenses here, ma'am" said Doc. Vince.

"Yeah! It's true. Your generosity now has already been compensated," added Doc Michael.

"I don't understand what are you saying! Please explain to me what does it mean?" Mila was already confused.

"When we were still young, we used to see you dropping coins in the donation box of the foundation where we stay. From then on, the three of us are always waiting for you every day in order to see you dropping your donation in that box. After that, we have made a promise that like what you do we will also help others when we grow," Doc Allan recounted to her.

"So you mean to say that you are one of the boys living in Santa Maria Foundation.? And also you," pointing her finger to Doc. Vince and Michael.

The three nodded.

"Wow! You're now a doctor. I'm proud of all of you, guys! Good job!"

"Thank you, ma'am."

"I am happy seeing you now as a successful doctor."

"We are also happy seeing you here, the one who dedicatedly donate a small amount for all of us orphans in the foundation. That's why you are now enjoying the copious fruits of your generosity. All your expenses are paid and you can stay here forever in the home for the aged."

"But I cannot pay all the fees here!" she said this because she was shocked that all her expenses were already paid.

"Don't worry we own this house and the hospital."

She said nothing but the tears fell down from her eyes, "Really! You're the owners of this house and the hospital?"

The three doctors smiled looking at her eyes crying. Then they approached her and hugged her tight.

Loving God, your love to us has become the reason for us to extend our hands towards our needy fellows. The fruit of this generosity becomes the chain of love because those who experiences the loving hands of others do the same towards others. Lord God, extend more this chain of love by drawing people to help so that the world may be filled with generous people who tirelessly help spread your love to humanity especially to people who need most of help. We lift up this prayer in the name of Jesus your Son who lives and reigns with You and the Holy Spirit, one God, forever and ever. Amen.

2

A Small Piece of Paper

"See that none of you repays evil for evil,
but always seek to do good to one another and to all."
1 Th 5:15

"Good morning Dr. Megs," cheered Ismael. Dr. Megs dela Torre was the director of Maria Dona Hospital and Ismael Carson was one of the utility staff of the hospital. It is his usual routine in the hospital that he extends his greetings to everybody with his warm smile. He had no family. He practically lived alone in his small house just nearby the hospital. No doubt, he had a lot of friends; doctors, nurses, patients, and utility staff, inside the hospital because of his warm attitude and kindness. The people liked him so much.

One thing which was enthralling to him was that he stopped before the patient's bed and mumbled words while closing his eyes, and then he left a small piece of paper on the small table beside the patient's bed and went on with his work.

One day, after cleaning the comfort room, he decided to drop by before the patient who was newly operated on with her breast cancer. He did the usual thing he does. The patient was alone because her watcher went downstairs to buy food. After he had finished, he picked up a small piece of paper and

7

placed it under the pillow of the patient. He was supposed to leave it on the table beside the patient, but he decided to leave it under her pillow. Suddenly, the watcher arrived and saw Ismael with his hands under the pillow of the patient. The lady shouted, "Thief! Thief! Thief!" It so happened that the wallet of the lady was under the pillow of the patient. And so, she was thinking that Ismael would be going to steal her money.

"No, Ma'am! It's not what you're thinking," he quaked. "I'm not a thief."

But the lady didn't heed him and went in haste to the director's office. Immediately after the report reached the hospital's director, Ismael was called to answer the accusation.

Five minutes later, he arrived at the office and the complainant was already there looking fiercely at him. He just bowed his head.

"Please have a seat, Ismael," Dr. Megs said. When he was already seated, Dr. Megs asked him directly, "Why did you steal, Ismael?"

When Ismael was about to answer, the lady interrupted, "I think my wallet is in his pocket."

Then Dr. Megs ordered Ismael to get what was inside in his pocket.

Ismael stood up and slowly took what was inside of his pocket. When he already got what was inside, he closed his hand and slowly placed it on the table of Dr. Megs. When he opened his hand, they saw a bundle of small papers. The lady and Dr. Megs were shocked. Then Dr. Megs picked up one and read what was within. He discovered that it was all about biblical quotations on the love and mercy of God towards his suffering people. The small piece of paper was a way of Ismael to encourage the patients and to remind them of the unconditional love and relentless mercy of God to them amidst of their sufferings.

The lady was in utter dismay at what she did to Ismael. She could not help but ask sorry for her rudeness towards Ismael. She regretted that she judge him immediately.

"I'm sorry, sir," the lady apologized. "I don't know what to say. I just realized that you're so good."

Ismael just smiled.

The whole incident had spread throughout the hospital and their curiosity was already answered.

Ever living God, teach us always to do good even in our own little ways, give importance to what is within us, value the things that give us eternal happiness. Thank you for giving us courage to go on with our lives despite the temptation of quitting doing good. Thank you for reminding us that giving is not about getting something in return but it is about giving ourselves to others without condition. We pray this through Christ who lives and reigns with You and the Holy Spirit, one God, forever and ever.
Amen.

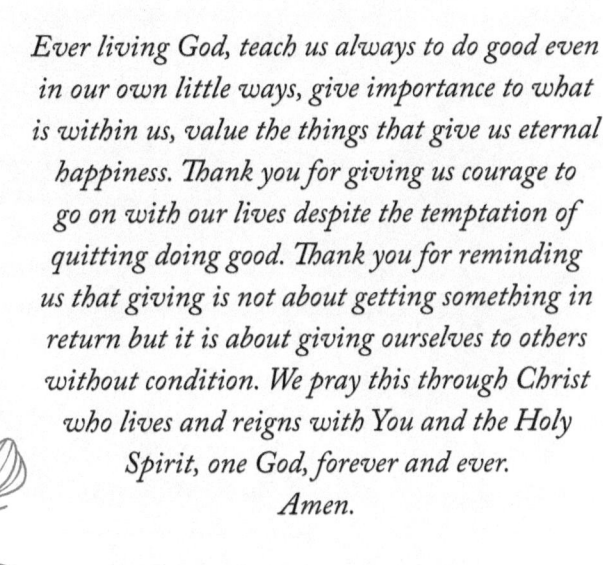

3

The Life I Live

"Of course, there is great gain in godliness with contentment."
1 Ti 6:6

Tano Selvano struggled to find his forever. He never dreamed of living alone. Part of his life-project was to marry his dream girl and established his own family. He was already sixty-five years old and still looking for his girl. He managed a small business, built his own house, and saved enough money for his future. Unfortunately, he was unlucky about his dream. He failed to reach it. He ended up alone. Sometimes, he asked God why He deprived him of his dream. But one thing beautiful happened in his life now was that he was contented with what he had. He just could not escape from the people's comments about his being single and alone. This had made him think why was it happening to him. He oftentimes heard from his neighbors that his life was so boring. He even overheard them talking about his life and his situation. He ignored them but their comments made him sad. He had understood from them that having your own family was the real measure of happiness.

However, his life was full of contentment and happiness. His sources of happiness came forth from his simple charity work; he usually visits orphanages for gift giving and bonding. He did it monthly when he could gather enough funds for his give-aways. In the beginning, he did it alone, but later on, he tapped his friends, relatives, and those generous people who were willing to support his charitable works. Indeed, he enjoyed doing it. This had made his life meaningful and happy.

He was confused when he heard those negative comments. Perhaps, he did not ask some wisdom from the religious person about this thing. But the puzzle of his confusion had totally arranged with one decisive occasion. One married man approached and praised his life.

"I envy your life now," Romeo, one of his acquaintances in his neighborhood, said.

"Why do you say so?" Tano replied.

"You look so happy even if you don't have your own family."

"I don't get what you mean? Tano was puzzled. "Are you not happy with your family?"

Romeo just remained silent. His face fell down and it was obvious that he was not happy. The shape of his face and his facial expression spoke of his sadness.

"I see. But why are they keep on telling me that living alone is boring and will lead to an unhappy life? I always heard from them that having your own family is heaven on earth. And now, you are telling me that you're not happy with your family."

"Yeah, I am not happy anymore," Romeo said. "My wife and I are always fighting and our children are already affected."

"Really! What happened?"

"I think, I don't love my wife anymore. I don't find meaning in my life anymore when I am with her."

"Is it really the reason for your fighting?"

Romeo nodded. "I think if I am single now, I can do whatever I want, and perhaps my life is full of meaning."

"I don't know if it's true."

"But I see in your eyes contentment and your life is meaningful."

"I don't know what to say and I'm wondering why you want my life now?"

"I just want your life now." Romeo then left him.

He was still puzzled about those things which Romeo had told him. He thought over it when he was home when he was lying on his bed. Then he realized that whatever status of your life, contentment, and happiness did not depend on it. It is the way we live out our lives that makes our life meaningful. It is how we express our love towards others that makes us happy and contented. His question was already answered; no need to have a family to live life to the full.

Gracious God, teach us to see beyond what the world has believed to be good. Help us transcend our judgemental eyes so that we may see the purpose of the lives of the people that we consider as a waste. Maybe for us it is a waste but for your eyes it is the mission that you have entrusted to them to do. That's why you have created us uniquely because your gift is diverse. I pray this through Christ who lives and reigns with You and the Holy Spirit, one God, forever and ever. Amen.

4

Crossing the Street

"So we can say with confidence, 'The Lord is my helper; I will not be afraid. What can anyone do to me.'"
Hebrew 13:6

"I will help you cross the street," Mang Eusebio offered help to the ten years old boy who was afraid to cross the street. Mang Eusebio looked like a beggar. He was so filthy and smelly. People might be afraid of him because of his appearance but many children still trusted him when he offered his help in assisting them to cross the street. He stayed just beside the gate of Esguerra Central Elementary School. He survived by receiving food or a small amount of money from the teachers of that school. He slept on the ground with his carton as his mattress and an empty sack of rice as his blanket. The teachers didn't know where was his whereabouts and his family. He just suddenly arrived there. They tried to inquire about his family, but unfortunately, they could not get the right answer because Mang Eusebio had a mental problem. And so they just stopped asking him about it and they just allowed him to help the children cross the street. At that time, there was no pedestrian lane and no enforcer who would assist the children crossing the street. And crossing the street was quite dangerous.

When the boy saw him smiling and extending his hand, he nodded and held his hand and they crossed the street altogether. When they were already on the other side of the road, the boy thanked him and rushed to the tricycle terminal.

Even though Mang Eusebio was already helping the students crossing the street, the teachers still pleaded with the Director of the school to approach the Government to establish the pedestrian lane and to assign one particular traffic enforcer to ensure the safety of the students. The Director found it urgent went to the Mayor's office and discussed it with him. Fortunately, the Government also believed that the problem had needed immediate action. So after three days, they installed the pedestrian lane and assigned one enforcer.

Monday morning, the enforcer was already on duty and ready to serve the children. But the children still approached Mang Eusebio to help them cross the street. When the enforcer saw them approaching him, he blew his whistle angrily. When the enforcer approached them, he suddenly pushed Mang Eusebio. His head was almost hit on the ground. He was hurt. The children pitied him and they helped him stand up.

"From now on you must use this pedestrian lane together with me as your guide," the enforcer demanded. "Never approach that beggar anymore! That's my job! That's why I am here."

Out of fear, the children followed the enforcer and they crossed the street through the pedestrian lane. Mang Eusebio bawled as he was looking at the children crossing the street with another guy.

From then on, he wailed and eat nothing for many days. The concerned teachers were already worried about him and his health. Unfortunately, after a week of not eating and always crying, he suddenly collapsed. And Sir Jonas, one of the concerned teachers, rushed him to the nearby hospital. After he was treated with Dextrose, he had slowly recovered. He was already conscious, but still crying. Then Sir Jonas discovered that Mang Eusebio was hospitalized at that medical center several times already. Indeed, he used to live in their home for the aged orphanage. However, he always escaped from the center and stayed on the street, especially nearby the school where he could help the children cross the street. Dr. Rivera, the attendant doctor of Mang Eusebio, recounted all this information to Sir Jonas.

"What is the story behind his desire to help the children in crossing the street?" Sir Jonas inquired.

"According to the reports, when he is still normal, he had three grandchildren. One time, he and his three grandchildren were playing football on the field. They really enjoyed doing it weekly. As his three grandchildren were playing, Mang Eusebio left them in order to buy snacks. But unfortunately, when he came back he found them lying dead on the road. They were hit by the garbage truck. According to some of the witnesses, one of them kicked the ball towards the direction of the road and the three followed the ball unmindful of the cars passing on the road," Dr. Rivera recounted.

"What a tragic accident," Sir Jonas sighed.

"Yeah! That's why he lost his mind," Dr. Rivera said. "The only thing has remained in his memory is the desire to help other children to be saved from possible hit and run incident in order to cover up the mistake he had done."

"I understand now why he is acting like that when the traffic enforcer pushed him and prohibited him to help the children," Sir Jonas recalled.

Meanwhile, Mang Eusebio still was not talking. He just stared blankly at the windows of his room. His recovery did not progress. He was sorrowful and crying all the time. When Sir Jonas witnessed this, it dawned in his mind a beautiful thought and whispered it to the ear of Mang Eusebio. While Sir Jonas was still whispering to him, his eyes shimmered in happiness. It seemed that there was magic that had spilled out from the mouth of Sir Jonas which had suddenly made him alive. After Sir Jonas whispered to him, he nodded as if he was saying yes to what they were agreeing for.

For this reason, Mang Eusebio had recovered rapidly. Indeed, one week later he was already discharged from the hospital. He was so excited to go back to school.

Because of curiosity, Dr. Rivera asked Sir Jonas what he had whispered to him which had made the recovery so fast, "What did you whisper to him?"

He grinned. Then he said, "I just told him he will be the assistant traffic enforcer in our school."

"Really!" Dr. Rivera beamed.

A week later after Mang Eusebio's discharge in the hospital, he then began his new job joyfully. Sir Jonas offered his house to Mang Eusebio and asked the city government to allow him to assist the enforcer in their school. He explained his reason to them and they happily allowed him to work and even offered a small compensation for him.

Lord God, you remind us that our goodness will remain forever. It does not fade away when we sin. But Lord, God, help us always to choose good amidst the bad situation of our lives. Hopefully, your love will push us to transcend our love for our brothers and sisters in order for us to love them without counting the cost. Our minds will forget the goodness we have done but our hearts who are full of love will never stop loving. This we pray through Jesus Christ who lives and reigns with You and the Holy Spirit, one God, forever and ever. Amen.

5

My Only One

"Yet for us there is one God, the Father, from whom are all things and for whom we exist, and one Lord, Jesus Christ, through whom are all things and through whom we exist."
1 Cor 8:6

Mr. Fred Delante was a successful sales manager at SanMis Corporation. He reached his status now because of perseverance and hardworking. Fortunately, the management paid for his dedicated work by promoting him constantly. He had almost everything in life except finding his only one. He was too focused on his job so much so that he forgot to find his love. Or he chose first his career over a woman. Several girls had expressed interest to be with him on a date. These girls were beautiful and wealthy. But he chose to drift away from them because he was happy without them in his life.

"Why are you still single?" asked Leny, one of his co-workers.

"I did not find yet my only one," Fred grinned.

"Yeah, I agree! You have already achieved the peak of your career. Now, it's time to settle down with your only one," Jeany, his other co-worker commented.

"Let us see," he smiled. "Who knows I will find her there."

"Where?" Leny and Jeany said in chorus.

"In Mirabe! We have to go now. It's already late. We will distribute groceries to our poor fellows there."

"Really! You can find nothing there," Leny discouraged him.

"We will go now! Let's talk about it some other time."

Mirabe was a poor place. The company chose this place as a recipient of its annual gift-giving. Usually, they give some groceries and rice to poor people. It is always part of the company's core values, to help the poor in simple and little ways. And Fred and his team were tasked to distribute the gifts.

An hour later, they arrived at Mirabe. It was quite distant from the city. Unexpectedly, the situation there was worst from what they had in mind. They were not only poor but the poorest of the poor. Some didn't have their own house but lived under the tree with their tent made up from the various materials of the garbage they had gathered. The children were mostly naked. They didn't have school. The situation was terrible. Seeing the situation of the people had made Fred remain silent. They then gathered the people for the distribution of the gifts they had brought. They did also a short program to entertain them before they would eat together with the food packs they had prepared.

Three hours later, they finally finished the whole program and the gift-giving. The people were happy and thankful for them. They could see in their eyes the joy of being graced by God through their generosity. But Fred still remained silent and said nothing during the course of their activity. The staffs were also happy as they departed from the Mirabe.

Two days later after their visit to Mirabe, Fred suddenly resigned from his job. He sent his resignation letter to his boss. The boss was shocked and did not accept the letter. He wanted that Fred would explain to him his reasons for quitting the job. However, Fred did not show up for fifteen days. Because of this, the management decided to accept his resignation and compensated him for the service he had rendered to the company. They did not know what happened to him. The company had lost a great man in their company. That's why it was hard for them to accept the reality that they lost perseverant employee. Even his colleagues couldn't understand why he resigned from his job. They were curious and sad about his decision. They were even sadder when they heard that he sold everything he had owned and left to nowhere. Now they didn't know where he stayed. No news of his whereabouts. He just suddenly disappeared.

One year later, when they had already forgotten Fred; when they have already accepted the reality that he was already gone, Fred appeared. He was on the Television. He was interviewed. Leny saw him on the T.V. during break time. She called the attention of all his co-workers and they all watched altogether the interview.

"Mr. Fred, welcome to my show," Mister Myer greeted and welcomed him in his show. His program was basically interviewing those people who were making an impact on society through their charity works. And Fred was interviewed because he was one of them.

"Thank you so much for inviting me here Sir Myer," Fred cheered.

"By the way, congratulations on winning the Novel Peace Award."

"Thank you."

"What makes you decide to leave everything and spend your time helping those poor people in Mirabe?"

There was a long pause of silence, "I still remember my first visit there."

"What do you remember there in your first visit?"

His colleagues were thrilled what he had remembered there in Mirabe which had made him decide to leave everything. Their eyes couldn't take off from the television.

"I found my only one."

"You mean to say that you have found the one who has made you fall in love, a woman in your life?"

He grinned. His colleagues were also intrigued. They were wondering who was that woman. When some of them went there, they didn't see any significant woman who captured the attention of Fred.

"No! it's not what you're thinking."

"Then what do you mean?"

"I saw in their eyes the one that I am looking for."

"What did you see in their eyes?"

"I saw in their eyes My one and only Lord."

Mr. Myer smiled gently after hearing him. His colleagues watching on the T.V. cried and had already understood his reason for leaving his comforts just to be with his One and Only. It is the Lord in the poor.

Loving God, the source of our joy, empty ourselves with the worldly riches which somehow lead us to greediness. Teach us to be generous by giving our whole selves. Teach us also to give without counting and expecting in return. We pray this through Christ who lives and reigns with You and the Holy Spirit, one God, forever and ever. Amen.

6

Commitment

"Every Sabbath day Aaron shall set them in order before the Lord
regularly as a commitment of the people of Israel, as a covenant forever."
—Leviticus 24:8

"I have to go!" Melanie Ental was determined to leave her husband Mark Ental. They were already married for five years but they didn't have a child. She worked as a company secretary of Sunglobe Communications Company. Mark Ental earned money as a manager of General Drugstore. Both were busy with their own job. That's why, after five years of married life, they were always fighting because they didn't have time for each other. Melanie would usually go home late at night. And Mark did the same. If Melanie went home early, Mark was not around. The same when Mark was around, Mary was outside enjoying the nightlife with her colleagues and boss.

"Why do you want to leave?" Mark asked.

Melanie just stared at him blankly.

Mark gripped her hands, "Did you find another man?"

She still said nothing. Then her tears dropped slowly on her cheek.

Mark cried after seeing her eyes guilty of his accusation, "I knew it! you don't need to tell me."

"Please let me go!" she begged. "Things will not work out for us anymore."

His knees slowly dropped on the floor as if his world collapsed. Then his whole body heavily descended on the ground and surrendered his sorrows on the bed of the world. Melanie left him lying on the floor and departed from their house. This time he did not stop her from leaving. He set her free. The pain had imprisoned him in the darkness of sadness. His suffering had been mixed with regrets for the times he failed to become a good husband. It was only now that he realized the value of the presence of his wife when she was already gone.

This is why Mark got lost in his life. He frequented the club together with his friends just to forget his wife and her infidelities. He is always late at the office. If he is just at home, he just stays in his room hiding in the darkness because all the windows were covered with thick and black curtains. There at the corner, he is always holding his phone checking the updates of his wife and spying on what is she doing. Unfortunately, his wife didn't post anything on her account on social media. His life during that year was a total mess.

Fortunately, after a year, he was already moved on with his life. Many aspects of his life have already come back to normal. However, fate is so playful sometimes. When he was already healed from the wounds of loneliness, when he was slowly retrieving the life that he somehow abandoned because of hopelessness, one incident has brought back the nightmares of his past. One time when he went to the grocery store to buy groceries for his personal consumption, he accidentally bumped a lady who was also buying groceries. The lady's groceries spilled on the floor. He then helped her to gather her groceries scattered on the floor and said, "I'm so sorry, ma'am." He did not look at the face of the lady and the lady also focused her attention on her groceries. When both of them finished picking up all the groceries, they stood up. When the lady turned her eyes to him and Mark also looked at her as if they looked at each other at the same time, both were shocked.

"Mark!" as if Melanie saw a ghost.

Mark looked so pale. His world stopped and his surroundings seemed to be in slow motion. He could not utter a single word.

Then Melanie smiled at him and asked, "How are you now?"

He just responded with a fake smile.

When Melanie sensed that he was not yet ready for that accidental meeting, she bid goodbye, "I have to go. Nice meeting you again, Mark." She then patted the shoulder of Mark and left.

Mark remained standing and did not turn his back to see her walking away. Melanie looked back and saw him still standing, not moving. She felt guilty seeing Mark was still not moving on. She whispered, "I'm so sorry."

However, after moments of standing there, he left his groceries and followed her. He kept his eyes on the car that Melanie was driving. He wanted to know where she was living and to see the person whom Melanie had replaced him with. After twenty minutes of travel, Melanie stopped in front of a simple apartment. He then pulled over his car twenty meters adjacent to Melanie's. She alighted the car with her groceries and entered the apartment. The door was wide open so much so that he could see the people inside. He saw three children: two boys and one girl. Their ages ranged from five to nine years old. It was already dark, and so, he decided to spy on what was inside the apartment. From the open window and the curtain was tied up and the light was on, he could see clearly what was happening inside. He was looking for a guy inside the apartment. He was already one hour outside but he did not see a guy. Only Melanie, who was busy cooking at the small kitchen, and the three children were inside.

But when Mark stepped a little forward on the window, he accidentally hit the flower pot and it fell on the ground. Then Melanie heard the sound of the broken pot. She grabbed her gun and went outside to check what was happening there. When she opened the door, she found out that one guy standing before the window looking inside the apartment. "Who are you?" while pointing the gun at him.

"No! Don't shoot me! It's me, Mark."

"Mark?!" She was flabbergasted. "What are you doing here?"

He did not say anything. He just vowed down his head.

Melanie was already calmed and asked him, "Please come inside."

Mark with hesitation followed her inside their apartment.

"Have a seat Mark."

He then seated on the couch uttering no words.

"What do you want? Coffee or juice?"

"Just give me coffee. Thank you."

Melanie prepared the coffee and served it to him. She sat before him staring at him while sipping the coffee.

"I know you hated me so much," she asserted. "I know that you have many things to ask me?"

He nodded. "Yes, I do!"

"This is the perfect time to ask me."

Without hesitation, he inquired, "Why do you leave me?"

Instead of answering him directly, she asked him, "Do you still remember when we were still together when I told him that I want to have a child?"

"Yes, I do."

"And you told me that you are not yet ready to become a father."

"Yes! That's why you left me because you want a baby," his voice raised a little. "You got what you want now with another man."

She nodded.

"How dare you!" he shouted. "You're so selfish!"

"If that is what you think, then I accept it."

Looking at the children who were outside playing under the street light, he inquired, "Are they your children?"

"Yes!"

"Worse than what I was thinking. You're already unfaithful a long time ago." While saying this he was looking at the children outside.

Instead of explaining about the children, Melanie shared the decisive moment which had made her decide to leave him. "One time I dropped by a Church to hear mass because at that time I was so stressed thinking our situation. And the desire to have our own children had hunted me. But you're not yet ready for it. Then during the homily, the priest said that marriage is not only about feeling or love and but above all, it is about God's love to His people. The couple is the living testament of this love. They are the reflection of God's love and His people. So our love reflects God's love when both of us are in love and most especially when are committed to each other to live the love of God in our lives. I don't know why I left you. I just realized that I have to go to give myself some space and for you to think about our marriage. I lived in the monastery for six months. There. I had found them. They are abandoned by their parents. And so I decided to adopt them. And the nuns were happy with my decision. Because of them, I worked hard and God was so generous. He gave me work that could sustain our needs. I wanted to go back with you, but I don't have the courage to do it because I heard of the news about leaving you with another guy. That is not true. I was wrong in thinking that you're not committed to our married life, but I am also to be blamed because I did not talk to you about my struggles and desires. I'm so sorry, Mark. I don't know if you could still forgive me."

Mark just sobbed. "I thought you were with another guy."

"No! I just want to be alone and think a moment. But because of what I've heard, I did not have the courage to come back."

Mark hugged his wife tightly and said, "I'm so sorry. Let us start again."

Melanie cried and hugged him too. "I'm sorry, too."

They started a new life with their three adopted children. After a year, God had blessed them with a lovely girl.

Loving God, source of beauty and goodness, strengthen our relationship with each other especially the love of each couple in the world. We pray that they may be always faithful towards their promises before You and the Church. May their love go beyond human limitations and expectations. May their commitment grow slowly as they grow older in their journey and their love may become a living testament of Your love towards humanity. We lift up this prayer through Christ who lives and reigns with You and the Holy Spirit, one God, forever and ever. Amen.

7

Two Boxes

"I have said this to you, so that in me you may have peace. In the world you face persecution. But take courage; I have conquered the world!"
John 16:33

The surrounding was so calm. The chirp of the birds was so melodious. She sat on the bench under the big acacia tree. She read closely the details of her notes. She studied hard during these days because the examination is fast approaching. She put on her earphones to aid her studies. She really found a nice place to study. Vanessa Retarde was a fourth-year accountancy student. She practically sustained her own study by selling anything like underwear, soap, RTW, and many more. She had also a part-time job in Jollibee near to her university school. Above all, she was a full-time scholar of Holy Rosary University. She was already orphaned when she was still fifteen years old. She just lived in the small apartment that she inherited from her father. So she lived there with her best friend, Alia Santos. She was also an orphan.

While seriously reading her notes and putting the maximum volume on her music, she heard a loud cry of a baby. She did not mind it. She remained focus on studying. But the cry of the baby has become louder. She took off her earphones to listen where the crying had come from. It was in the forest part of the plaza. But she did not mind it again and continued her studying. This time the crying of the baby was doubled. It became stronger and louder. It seemed that two babies were crying in unison.

She dropped her notes on the bench, removed the earphones, and slowly paced towards the forest. The sound of the cry, probably, was twenty meters away. She listened to the cry and followed in that direction. After minutes of walking, she saw two boxes wrapped with electrical tape. She stopped before them. She then slowly unboxed them. She was so shocked after seeing what was within, a lovely and beautiful baby. She then opened the other box. Another baby was inside the box; a lovely and beautiful baby. She placed the two babies side by side and concluded that they were twins.

"Oh my, God! What should I do with them?" she was already trembling and confused. She then phoned her best friend, Alia, and asked her to come and see what she had found.

Thirty minutes later, Alia arrived.

"What happened?" Alia inquired. She looked so worried.

"Come over here!"

Alia followed her at the back of the big acacia tree. There she saw the two lovely babies.

"Wow!" she was so happy after seeing the two lovely twins. "They're really cute!" She caressed their cheeks.

"They're so lovely, isn't it?" Melanie commented.

"Yeah!" Alia agreed. "Anyway! Where are their parents?"

"I don't know."

"What? You don't know!"

"Yes, I really don't know."

"Then where did you find them?"

"I saw them there in the forest," She said. "I just heard their cries while I was studying my notes. When I checked who was crying, I discovered them inside the two boxes."

"Okay," Alia was still in doubt. "What should we do now?"

"I don't know."

"Let us bring them to the police."

"Yeah, It's a good idea."

"Let's go now."

While on the way to the police station, it suddenly dawned on Vanessa the idea of adopting them.

"Wait! Vanessa shouted at the taxi driver.

"Why?" Alisa inquired.

"Let us talk it when we are already alighted off from the taxi," she explained.

Alia nodded, but she was still confused.

When they were already off from the taxi and fortunately had found a place to speak, Vanessa then broke out to her what she wanted to tell her. "I want to adopt them."

"What? Are you insane?"

"No! I just don't want them to be orphaned."

"The police officer will take charge of everything about the twins."

"I know, but I want to raise them myself."

"We can't do that. We are still studying and no one will take care of them when we are at school."

"Let us bring them to school."

"Are you insane? We can't do that."

"We can," Vanessa insisted.

"What are you thinking?" Alia doubted. "They will not allow us to bring them to our class. Besides, they will think we are single parents. They might talk about us on our backs. Our reputation at school will be ruined."

"I know, but I don't care what they say," she was really determined. "I am sure of what we are going to do. It is risky and shameful. But I have decided already, are you in or not?

Alia paused awhile and seemed she was nervous and afraid of what they are going to do. But she said yes to her. "Okay let's do it."

"Thank you so much!" Vanessa hugged her.

They took turns taking care of the babies. If Vanessa has class, Alia will take care of the twins. Vanessa will take charge of them when Alia has classes. Fortunately, both have different classes schedules. However, they had difficulty sustaining the basic needs of the twins. Because of this, they saved the money intended for their snacks. Above all, they already felt the fruits of having the twins in their lives: they became the subject of the gossip in their universities, they didn't have suitors, their classmates considered them as slut, and many other false accusations. That's why Alia could no longer stomach the negative comments she has always heard from school and their neighborhood, she opted to leave without bidding goodbye to her bestfriend. She stayed with her auntie. Vanessa was feeling down after she had found out that her bestfriend left her. She didn't know what she was going to do with the twins and her life. She could not raise the twins alone. Until she decided to turn over the twins to the Department of Social Welfare and Development. That was the only and best way, she thought, for the twins to have a good life at that particular moment of her struggles. But when she was already in front of the office of DSWD, she suddenly changed her mind and went back to her apartment. She already loved the twins like her own children. She could not let them be away from her life.

Even if it was difficult having the twins in her life, she was determined to raise them. She usually brings them inside her class. And so, her classmates helped her in taking care of the twins. Her classmates were enjoying babysitting the twins. Indeed, also their professors extended their help financially to her. They also were having fun when the twins were inside the classroom. Because of them, she was able to raise them without so much difficulty.

Finally, she already harvested the fruits of her labor. She is now going to receive her certificate of graduation as Cum Laude. During the graduation rites, the twins were in the hands of the professors while she was receiving her medals and certificate. In her valedictory address, she thanked all who had been so generous in helping her study, especially in extending their hands for the twins' needs. She said that having children while studying was not a hindrance to pursuing their dreams. After her speech, the people stood up while giving their joyous applause. They still believed that the twins were her children. She did not tell her about the truth. But what was important to her now was that she was able to shout out in the world that being a single mother was a privilege, not a curse; not a hindrance, but a blessing to pursue their dreams.

Grant us, oh Lord, the courage to fight against all odds. Increase our courage when we are down because of problems, difficulties, and sufferings. May our determination and love for the service of others prevail over the swords of evil in the world. We entrust to you our whole self in Jesus' name who lives and reigns with You and the Holy Spirit, one God, forever and ever. Amen.

8

Money Can Give Us Happiness

"In the days of Shalmaneser I performed many acts of charity
to my kindred, those of my tribe."
Tobit 1:16

Felmark Martil, at a young age, already owned a Shoe Company. His grandfather, Mario Martil, exposed him to the business world when he was a teenager. Mario trained him how to run a business and gave some techniques on how to do them. That's why his success is attributed to his grandfather. Unfortunately, Mario died at the peak of his success and was left an orphan. Mario missed the fortune that Felmark had gained. He topped the richest people in his country. However, he had no one around who would share in his success. Mario, his only family, had gone forever and he remained single.

Indeed, loneliness visits him everyday after the death of his grandfather. It just comes and goes and comes again when he is alone in his luxurious house. His heart was covered with discontentment. His mind fixated on buying luxurious cars. But his life swamped all the more in the flood of loneliness and discontentment. As people said, "Money can't buy happiness." This saying manifested in his life. He looked at something beyond what money could give, happiness that could fill in the empty space of his life.

His restlessness steered him to go to his rest house adjacent to the sea. He owned a magnificent and huge beach resort. He opted to do rest from his routine and unwind, savoring the fresh breeze of the air, unloading the negativity of the city, and adoring the beauty of creation. But, before reaching the place, a terrible view could hack the beauteous and scenic panorama of the beach. A slum area heisted the nobility of the place. Malnourished children hovered the slum. The houses were built up from the different garbage they collected from the roads. They were like the cage of the swine. The face of poverty was seen on the face of the people living there.

Passing on that place, he realized how the people had needed the wealth he had possessed. They were so poor. Even eating three times a day, they could not afford. He sensed their struggle by looking directly into their eyes. He then moved with pity for them. He said to himself, "What should I do with them?"

This question encroached on the deepest being of himself. He brought it along with his loneliness and discontentment. Instead of relaxing on the beach, his time is spent on reflecting what he should do with the poor people. He did it for a week, then he decided to reach out to them. He conducted a meeting with the staff he created in order to actualize his plan. The group decided to give them their basic needs once a month and they gave each family a fund for their small business. But before giving it to them, they conducted a series of seminars on how to do small business and the techniques of profiting from it.

His world revolved not only for his company, but he was busy doing charity. He then slowly felt happiness which comes from within. His constant visitor left him already. He vowed not to welcome them anymore. It had no space in his life now. As he looked around the place, his staff were busy doing their jobs, the smiles of the people were priceless, he said, "Money, indeed, can buy happiness when it is spent to others."

Loving and merciful God, source and fountain of love, draw us always to Your loving presence so that we may learn to love you by loving others. We thank You for the great mercy You have shown upon us. May this experience become an inspiration for us to live in love and be a living witness of this love. We pray this through Christ who lives and reigns with You and the Holy Spirit, one God, forever and ever. Amen.

9

Great Silence

"Let the elders who rule well be considered worthy of double honor, especially those who labor in preaching and teaching."
1 Ti 5:17

Usually after the mass, the parishioners of Fr. Rex Gutala hovered around him to give each their compliment. He was so creative and articulate in his homily. One said, "Fr. Rex, your homily is so inspiring." Some others said, "You have a very touching homily, Fr. Rex." These words resounded in his ears every after the mass. Fortunately, they could gather after the mass because Fr. Rex had no other mass during Sunday and the parish belonged to a small town of the municipality of Magsaysay. The population reached only 1,000 families. And so, they spent some time after the mass praising Fr. Rex, commenting fascinating words.

He prepared well his homily. In his seminary days, the formators and seminarians already observed his expertise in the Scriptures. He explained well the backgrounds of the texts. He articulated his reflection about the texts in an exegetical way but understandable to ordinary people. He was happy with the positive comments of his parishioners. This made him inspired to make his homily livelier and more interesting.

As the days had gone by, he noticed that people during the celebration of the mass talked a lot. The noise elated every Sunday. They hardly observed the great silence in the mass. He then concluded that their positive comments contradicted their action inside the celebration. "If they are moved with my homily, it should be seen in their actions. They should be in the prayer mode," he pensively said to himself.

He also noticed that they became back fighters. He discovered it when they had informal conversations. Instead of commenting about his homily, they talked about the life of others. He tried to ignore them by diverting their topic. He hoped that someday they may change their ways and that they might live their identity as Christians. However, as their life went on, they had become worse. The noise inside the church had been alarming. Their respect for the sanctity of the church deteriorated. The silence had been denied. Their virulent words against their neighbors escalated and reverberated in the ears of Fr. Rex. The bad tune of the people almost destroyed the eardrum of Fr. Rex's faith in them. This led him to worry about his flocks. He was also frustrated because he expected that his homily helped them in living out their Christian faith. But what they showed was the other way around.

Frustration hammered the head of his expectation. He could not breathe of its pain. The wound was unbearable on his journey as a priest and pastor. He then frequented the oratory of their convent to pray, outpouring to God all his disappointments and frustrations. He also asked God for enlightenment on his problems. Of course, God sometimes didn't answer our prayer clearly and immediately. It takes time sometimes. But the only thing that always enters his mind is the idea of home visitation of his parishioners. He didn't know that it would be the solution to his problems. But he liked to do it in order to know them better. And since the parish was just small, it is possible to do it. He scheduled two hours of daily visitation to random families. Shock and surprise were the reactions of the people he had randomly visited. But certain happiness unfolded on their eyes and blossomed on their lips with their delightful smiles. Because of this, Fr. Rex established a personal relationship with them, based not only on a casual level but on an emphatic degree of relating. He dug deeper into their personal life. And the parishioners knew slowly their pastors. And then after home visitation, he confided everything to God in prayer. This had become his daily routine.

In his homily, he already changed his style; from too exegetical to a more experiential homily. It meant that his homily was blended with exegetics and experiential which somehow touched the lives of his flocks. He was able to connect the gospel message to the struggles, joys, and hope of the people. And then what was a significant revelation he had observed to the people during the mass was that they already observed silence. They seemed to be reflective during the entire celebration. He also wondered why they no longer approached him after the mass and expressed their compliments. They simply smiled at him but their faces shine in happiness.

One occasion after his mass, one stranger approached him and said, "You know Fr. Rex, my wife is no longer back fighting our neighbor. She is very different now. I don't know what happens. I think it's because of the depth of your homily."

"What do you mean by depth?" He asked.

"I noticed now that your homily is already grounded in our reality."

"I don't understand what you mean?"

"You are full of ideas Fr. Rex. That is what I noticed before in your homily."

"Really! Thank you for your observation."

"But now you don't have only ideas, you have already depth. You can connect now to the ordinary lives of the people; their experiences so on and so forth. I think that's the reason why my wife has changed."

"Oh really! I hope it's true."

The man beamed and bid goodbye to Fr. Rex.

"Perhaps that's the answer to my prayer," he said to himself.

He realized that his homily lacked depth. He achieved depth through entering the ordinary lives of his people. That's the result of his perseverance in-home visitation. He was now connected with the peoples' lives. His homily had impacted his parishioners. A good preacher was not enough, but he must be a good pastor.

Lord God, Almighty, may your loving presence fills our life with your love and help us to radiate this to others. May we become a living witness of your love to others by our own examples and life. May our preaching become our life. We lift up this through Christ, our Lord, who lives and reigns with You and the Holy Spirit, one God. Forever and ever. Amen.

10
Jeepney

"There is the gift that profits you nothing, and the gift to be paid back double."
Sirach 20:10

All his things were packed up in one big piece of luggage. All were already set, but Rayly and his family were not yet ready for his leaving. Lyra, his wife, was sad while watching him wearing his shoes. They had no choice; the increasing demand of their two college children was their priority and the opportunity to work in Dubai cohered with their needs. His salary here in the Philippines was not enough. When he and his wife came out from their room, their children, Mat, and Chea were already crying. Lyra also cried after seeing them weeping. Rayly held his tears; he tried to be strong for them.

"I have to go now," Rayly said. "Please take care of your mom, Mat."

Mat nodded while still crying. He was his eldest son.

"Honey, please take care of yourself and our children." He then hugged his wife.

"Yes! I will," Lyra said.

Rayly approached his children and hugged them one by one and told them to study hard, behave well and take care of themselves and their mother.

The Jeepney 1960 model waited outside their residence. Roberto, the uncle of Rayly, owned it. Instead of a taxi, they rented it in order to save. He loaded his luggage and they departed with his wife and children to the airport.

They departed at 7:00 a.m. and his flight was still at 11:00 a.m., good enough to reach the airport early. However, last night was pouring. Muddy and slippery road slowed down the Jeepney. Sometimes, the Jeepney is stuck in the mud. Roberto's experience and skill in driving helped them overcome all those obstacles. One hour later of their struggle, they finally reached the highway. It was already 8:00 a.m. The estimated travel time from the highway to the airport was one hour and a half. Due to Jeepney's condition and age, they probably arrived at the airport two hours later.

While on the highway, they passed by two men fixing their car. Rayly, known as a helpful man, he tapped the shoulder of Roberto and told him to stop. He approached the men. One was wearing a black polo shirt and blue jeans. He was a good-looking guy in his fifties. It was obvious that he was rich. The other guy was the driver, he guessed because he wore a uniform for the private driver.

"Good morning, sirs?" he greeted them. "Is there any problem?"

"Good morning, too, sir," said the good-looking guy. "The engine just suddenly stopped. We don't know what happened."

"Let me check your car, sir, if it is okay with you?"

"Yes, of course."

Rayly checked the engine of his car. Then he saw that the host where the gasoline passes going to the engine was cut-off.

"I think, I found already the problem with your car, sir." Rayly said.

"Really! What is the problem?" asked the good-looking guy.

"The hose where the gasoline passes going to the engine was cut-off."

"Oh my goodness! How does it happen?"

"Perhaps, someone has intentionally cut it out."

"Really! I will find out who did it."

"By the way, sir, where are you going?" Rayly asked him.

"I am heading to the airport."

"Oh! We are also going there. If you want sir, you can join us."

"If it is just okay with you, yes I will," he said.

"Yes, of course, sir! There is still space. But our Jeepney is already old. Please bear with our vehicle."

"There is no problem with me as long as I can reach the airport on time because I have an important meeting abroad."

"Okay, sir, let's go now."

"Okay. Thank you so much."

Rayly then helped the guy carry his luggage and loaded it in the Jeepney.

They arrived at the airport at exactly 10:15 a.m. The guy alighted off from the Jeepney and thanked him for his help and for the ride. Rayly also alighted off from the Jeepney and bid goodbye to his children and his wife with a big hug and kissed each one of them. All of them shed tears, but he must go. He rushed to the check-in counter in order to catch up on his flight. It was already the last boarding call. Fortunately, he made it and flew to Dubai.

After four hours of traveling, he finally arrived in Dubai. One guy from the company picked him up at the airport and dropped him at the five-star hotel. The guy told him to have some rest for tomorrow's interview. He then rested and enjoyed the luxury of the hotel. His schedule would be at 9:00 a.m. At 8:00 a.m., he took the elevator from the 10th floor to the 20th floor. On the 12th floor, the elevator stopped. The good-looking guy whom he helped entered the elevator.

"Hello, sir!" Rayly was so surprised seeing him in the elevator.

"Oh! What are you doing here?" the guy was also taken aback.

"I'm here for work, sir. Today is my interview."

"Ah! Really! What a small world," the guy grinned.

"Yeah! I just met you yesterday in the Philippines, but now I see you here in Dubai."

"By the way, thank you again for your help. I was able to catch up with my schedule yesterday because of your generosity."

"Your welcome, sir. By the way, sir, what are you doing here?"

The guy didn't answer him because someone phoned him.

"I have to go now. I'm so sorry," the guy said while rushing out to the elevator.

He proceeded to the interview. It took only half an hour. He wondered why the interviewer did not tell him about his job. He only asked him some irrelevant questions. And then, the interviewer told him to come back tomorrow.

At exactly 8:00 a.m. of the next day, he waited already in the office. Fifteen minutes later, the interviewer came.

"Good morning, sir," The interviewer said. "Thank you for waiting."

"It's okay, sir," he replied.

"Regarding your assigned work, I have already here your job assignment and the place of your assignment. The Boss hired you as a manager of a convenience store and your monthly salary will be thirty-five thousand pesos."

"Oh my, God!" He was so shocked.

"Congratulations!" The interviewer shook his hand. "But you have to go back to the Philippines tomorrow. Your ticket is here already."

"But why, sir?" He reacted.

"You'll work there, of course. Don't you want the job?" The interviewer said. "By the way, I have to go now. I have a meeting. Congratulations once again!" The interviewer then handed the ticket to him and went.

Rayly, still recovering from bewilderment, came out. When he was already outside of the office, he saw the good-looking guy at the huge office before him. He was seated on the big chair. The guy also saw him and waved his hand to him.

Because of curiosity, Rayly asked one guy he had met at the isle, "Who is that man at the big office."

The man replied, "He is the owner and CEO of the company."

*Loving God and generous Father, you have
taught us how to be generous towards all
the people in need. Help us always to show
our generous love to all the people in every
circumstance of our lives. We may always share
the love we have received from you in our own
little ways. And by sharing it, may the people
who have received it would do the same. We
pray this through Christ who lives and reigns
with You and the Holy Spirit, one God, forever
and ever. Amen.*

⤳ 11 ⤲

100 Pesos

"And one of you says to them, 'Go in peace; keep warm and eat your fill,'
and yet you do not supply their bodily needs, what is the good of that."
James 2:16

I drove an L300 Mitsubishi Car when I passed a quiet road. Fifty meters away from me, I saw one boy, aged ten to twelve years old, made a hitchhiking sign. I was hesitant. Many incidents of robbery had been reported on that road. There was a fight between my heart and mind. But my heart won the battle. I pulled over the car at the side and the boy rode with me.

"Where are you going, boy?" I asked.

"At Manticao!" he said. Manticao was five kilometers away from that place. It's a wet market.

"By the way, what is your name?"

"I'm Rover!" After that, he remained silent. He looked so worried.

"What are you going to do in Manticao?"

Rover didn't answer me. He was unmindful of my question.

"I'll go to my sister's house," he finally talked.

"Ah Okay."

He was sad. I can see in his eyes a pain, brokenness.

"I am so hungry."

I didn't say anything. I just wanted him to talk.

"I and my mother didn't eat yet."

"It's already 1:30 P.M. and you didn't eat yet."

He nodded.

"Why?"

"There is no food." I noticed that he tried to hold his tears from falling. His face was morose. He breathed deeply.

I just simply nodded. I did not say anything but within my heart was the pain of seeing him suffering. It was almost noon but he did not eat yet and his mother. He reminded me of my own experience when my family had nothing to eat at that time. I can bear the hunger but seeing my family hungry, I was dejected and suffering. I had felt what Rover had experienced. We can bear the hunger, but seeing our family suffer was unbearable.

"Just drop me at the side, sir!" Rover said.

"Okay!"

"By the way, sir, what is your name?" he asked.

"Recky," I said. I then picked up the one-hundred-peso bill inside my pocket and handed it to him, "I hope it could help!" That's the money I had at that time.

His face glowed shortly after seeing the one-hundred-peso bill. His lips opened a little as if he wanted to smile but he was hesitant. His eyes were teary. He didn't utter a single word. He just gazed on the one-hundred-peso bill. Looking at him, I almost cried. It was a great and golden experience. He looked at me and smiled, "Thank you so much!" He then waved his hands. I waved back as I slowly speed up the wheel.

Indeed, that encounter of simple listening and a gesture of giving a small amount is heaven on earth. I was able to give my all in a small amount simply because I knew the pain he went through at that time. His situation had reflected my own experience with my family.

One week later, I saw him again on that same road. He smiled at me when he saw me. We talked. This time he was energetic and enthusiastic in his sharing. Everytime I passed on that road, I always see him, and we talked a lot, and we became friends.

Lord God, may You give us the eyes to see the needs of our needy brothers and sisters. Make our own pains an avenue to help them with a pure and sincere heart. Help us to carry the mission of spreading Your love towards our brethren. We may not stop showing it even if we are also struggling to live out our identity as Your sons and daughters. We pray this through Christ who lives and reigns with You and the Holy Spirit, one God, forever and ever. Amen.

12

Listen First

"Like a gold ring or an ornament of gold is a wise rebuke to a listening ear."
- Proverbs 25:12

Eric Mata was waiting for Karen, her daughter, at the terrace of their house. It was already 11:00 p.m. She didn't arrive yet from school. He was already anxious. He phoned her several times but she was out of the coverage area. He was not only anxious, but he also was angry. He cared and loved her daughter so much since she was the only child. Eric became a widower when Karen was still one-year-old. His wife died from breast cancer. That's why he protected her from all harm. He didn't want to lose her after his wife's death. He did not even marry again so that he could focus his attention on her. He gave everything to her. Fortunately, Karen grew with the virtues of kindness, humility, obedience, loving, and perseverance. She has never disappointed her father. She also loved her father very much.

At 12:00 midnight, Karen arrived home. She looked so afraid. She did not look at her father's eyes. Her innocent cheeks were filled with tears. She even trembled as if she will be sentenced to death and she was already marching towards the death chamber. Eric stood near the door looking at her daughter.

When Karen was already in front of her father, she wept. Eric then hugged her and kissed her forehead.

"I'm sorry, dad," she said.

Eric hugged him tightly and said, "Have you eaten your dinner already, honey?"

"Not yet dad," she was somehow relieved because Eric was so calm.

"Put your things inside your room and we will eat together." Then he prepared their dinner and ate together. During their meal, both of them did not utter a single word. Eric was allowing her daughter to eat her dinner peacefully. Karen felt ashamed for what she had done and still afraid of him. But Eric smiled whenever she would look at him. She also smiled back but was a bit hesitant. After they took their dinner, they did the dishes together. And then after dishwashing, Eric asked her, "Can we talk?"

Karen was so pale when her father asked this. She nodded. But her eyes were already reddish. The tears were ready to burst out into her eyes and would eventually create a small river on her cheeks. The situation became worse when she saw her luggage outside her room. She remembered before that her father told her that she will be sent out if she would disappoint him. While Eric was putting the two pieces of her luggage in order, she cried on the couch. Eric was so serious.

"By the way, honey, why are you late?" he asked this while he was busy arranging the luggage.

She immediately stood up and wept, "I am sorry, dad," her voice was stuttering.

"Oh! What happen?" he asked. "Are you all right?"

"Don't send me away. Promise I won't be late anymore."

"No! I will not do it. Why should I?"

She stopped crying when he heard her father. "But my luggage is already here. I just remember before that you told me if I disappoint you, you will send me away," she explained.

He grinned, "I can't do that! You know that I love you."

This time she smiled. "But why is it that my luggage is here?"

He laughed. "I just wanted to borrow it from you because the next day we will have an out-of-town meeting," he said. "Anyway, I just still need to ask you about this, why are you late?"

"I got stocked up from the floods in the city, dad," she reasoned. "The battery of my Cellphone was already dead."

"Ah okay! That's what I wanted to ask you because I am so worried about you."

"Sorry, dad."

"It's okay. Don't worry I am not angry with you. Just make sure that next time you can communicate with me. Okay?"

"Yes, dad. I will find ways to do it."

Then, Eric hugged her daughter, and that night they slept peacefully.

Usually, in our life, we reacted to bad situations negatively. Instead of listening first to the explanation of others, we immediately conclude and won't listen to their explanation.

Loving and merciful God, you always listen to the cry of the poor. Pour forth your Spirit upon us so that we may be able to listen first before we judge others. We pray that we may gradually learn the secrets of listening before we talk. Especially teach us to pray in a manner of listening to your will in the silence of our hearts and minds. We ask this through Christ who lives and reigns with You and the Holy Spirit, one God, forever and ever. Amen.

13

Loving is the True Gauge of Mission

"For if I do this of my own will, I have a reward;
but if not of my own will, I am entrusted with a commission."
– 1 Cor 9:17

Fr. Dave Wenslao, the General Superior of Divine Mercy Missionary visited Fr. Vic to their mission in Diwata. Fr. Vic was the priest-in-charge of the mission and he served the locals of the place. It was a far-reaching place, had a difficult road, inaccessible for any vehicles, and was located in the middle of the forest. They had to walk six hours, cross rivers many times, and climb high mountains before reaching the proper place. They had a small school, a chapel, and a livelihood program. Derio, the elder of the locals, accompanied Fr. Dave on his journey to Diwata. Fr. Vic asked him to be his guide. While waiting for their visitor, Fr. Vic had prepared a simple celebration for the General Superior as their way to welcome him. The purpose of the visit was pastoral: to know the situation of the mission and to show support for Fr. Vic's mission. The mission in Diwata was officially opened last two years ago and Fr. Vic was the first missionary.

Finally, after a long and arduous journey, Fr. Dave arrived. He witnessed the welcoming spirit and undaunting hospitality of the people with the festivity that they had prepared for him. After a while, they began the simple celebration by eating together. The locals performed their traditional dance. Fr. Dave rejoiced with their performance and forgot the exhaustion of their long journey. Their jovial dancing even made him dance with them. When the festive celebration had ended, they all rested in their respective huts.

On the next day, Fr. Dave conversed with Fr. Vic about the mission and his mission with them.

"How are you, Fr. Vic?" Fr. Dave asked.

"I'm good," he replied.

"I'm happy seeing you here surviving all the hardships of the mission," he then patted his shoulder. "How's your mission here?"

Without hesitation, he said, "I am so frustrated because from the time I arrived here there is no improvement of their lives even though I did already what I was supposed to do, but nothing happens."

Fr. Dave sighed and said, "If I might interpret from what you've said to me, you're looking for the result of all that you have done to them."

"Of course!" he confidently replied. "That's always what we're looking for in everything we do."

"Yeah! I agree with you," Fr. Dave said. "We need to measure the results of what we're doing, but the most important thing that we should do in mission is to do what we supposed to do as of right. And in doing the right thing is to relate, to love, to immerse in their lives, and be part of their lives as one among them in their struggles, hope, joy, and victories. Because if we will go directly to seeing the measurable results, we will indeed end up disappointed and frustrated. You measure the result of your mission not only looking for the improvement of the lives of the people entrusted to you but most importantly, seeing your growth when you are with them. Do you grow in loving? Do you learn to be generous in giving your whole self to them? Do you notice that you become loving when you're with them compared with your previous life? This is, I think, the best measurement we can use in order to know the effectiveness of our mission."

Fr. Vic did not utter a single word. But he realized that Fr. General was absolutely right.

"I invite you to begin your mission here with this idea I propose. Let us see what will happen," Fr. Dave brotherly suggested to him.

"Thank you so much, Fr. Dave, for your advice."

The General Superior then gave him a big hug and said, "Just trust me it will work because Jesus had exemplified it."

The General Council knew Fr. Vic was always looking for good results of whatever mission entrusted to him. This was his struggle as a religious. To address this problem, the General Council decided to send him on this mission. The plan was to help him learn to be loving with ordinary people he was serving; to refocus his attention from a result-oriented person to a loving person and his mission.

Loving God, help us to begin our mission with love, not by looking for the results. We may do it faithfully and wholeheartedly so that we may become effective and fruitful missionaries in Your vineyard. We pray this through Christ who lives and reigns with You and the Holy Spirit, one God, forever and ever. Amen.

14

She is in Heaven

"But they will have to give an accounting to him
who stands ready to judge the living and the dead."
1 Peter 4:5

Dorothy Intal was the CEO of the New York Laundry Company. Her employees considered her as a strict boss, a nagger old lady, and a boring mistress. That's why she was the favorite subject of the gossip inside the company. They talked a lot behind her back.

Indeed, we do not know the end of our lives. Death is inevitable. It comes sometimes when we don't expect it. On one occasion, Dorothy and her managers flew to Cebu City for their three-day seminar. When they were already up there, one of the engines of the airbus failed and eventually crashed on the sea. Unfortunately, all the passengers died.

As we believe, all the worthy souls after dying will go directly to heaven. And so, Dorothy and her managers met in heaven. St. Peter welcomed them. When one of the managers of Dorothy saw her in heaven, he secretly approached St. Peter and asked, "Sir, if you don't mind, I would just like to ask you one question. I am just curious."

Then Peter replied. "No, I don't mind. What is your question, my dear?"

"I would just like to ask why is it that my boss is here in heaven with us? She was so rude at us back on earth."

St. Peter paused for a moment while looking to the one asking him a question. Then he said, "You know, my dear, we judge her based on her charity. She always goes to the orphanages and houses of the old-aged foundations to share his love. She spent her time playing and conversing with them. She didn't only offer material things for them, but she shared her love and time for them. Back at her home, she has a lot of pets and she adopted abandoned animals. She is full of love. Her love extended towards the animals which we usually forget on earth. You have many things which you don't know about her. I think, what have you experienced with her on earth is part of her weaknesses. And you chose to be nailed on this belief."

They were now enlightened and happy to know her better.

Loving and merciful Father, give us eyes to see what is beyond our eyes can see, a heart that is willing to love beyond the criteria of the world. Teach us to be generous in pouring our love towards others. We ask this through Christ who lives and reigns with You and the Holy Spirit, one God, forever and ever. Amen.

15

Picture Frame

"You are not ignorant of the affection of family ties, which the divine and all-wise Providence has bequeathed through the fathers to their descendants and which was implanted in the mother's womb."
- 4 Macc 13:19

There was a loud pounding in the other room. The noise of fighting had awakened Madel. She stood up and ran to the room of her mother and her live-in partner. She then discovered that Elena, her mother, and Diego, her mother's partner, were fighting. She shouted at them, "Stop!" The couple halted from fighting after they had heard Madel shouting. The sun would not arise if the couple stop fighting every morning. This had become a daily routine for them. The reason for fighting was jealousy. Diego got jealous of all the people that Elena had acquainted: on the street, on the market, and even their neighbors.

Madel kept on reminding her mother to leave Diego, but she refused because they had nowhere to go and Diego sustained their life. Madel could not help but cried in her room holding the picture frame of her late father, Marcelo. Her father was a policeman. He died five years ago after he was shot dead during the raid of the most notorious drug lord in the city. That picture frame remained the sole remembrance of her father. She usually unloads her pains in front of her father's picture.

Emoting in her room, she heard again a loud bang in the other room. "They're fighting again," she thought. She got up and ran fast to the other room. What she saw in their room shocked her. Diego jabbed Elena like a punching bag.

"Stop it!" she shouted.

Diego listened to her and stopped beating Elena.

Madel helped her mother stand up and said, "We'll leave this house, mom!"

"We can't do that, Madel!"

"But why can't we do it?"

"You know already the reason."

As usual, Madel entered her room and cried with the picture frame. But another chaos she had heard in the other room. Of course, she checked again bringing along with her the picture frame. When she opened the door, she was flabbergasted seeing Diego with a sharp knife in his hand who was about to stab Elena. Madel then smashed the picture frame into the head of Diego. She hit him hard so much so that he fell unconscious on the ground.

While watching Diego lying on the floor, she saw something; it was a bank book and a check which already had a signature. She grabbed it and browsed. She found out that the money deposited in it worth one million pesos. She cried seeing it and showed it to her mother. They both cried. Then the police officers arrived. The concerned neighbor called them to rescue them from the danger.

Finally, Diego already served his crime in the prison. Madel and her mother lived a new chapter of their lives with the money which his father had left them.

Merciful God, grant us always the grace to find you amidst our troubled moments and calmed days. We hopefully see good things in the bad situation of our lives which we may encounter along our journey. But your constant providence reminds us of your superabundant love for all of us. This I pray through Christ who lives and reigns with You and the Holy Spirit, one God, forever and ever. Amen.

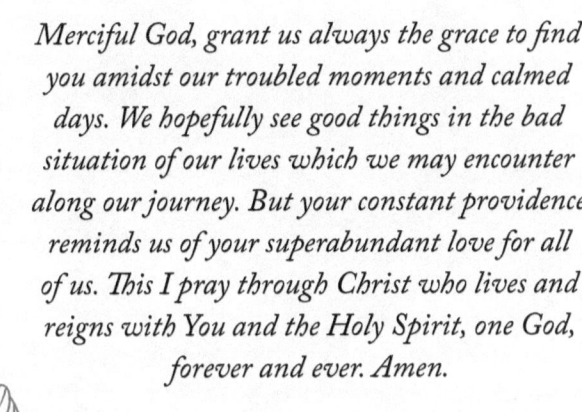

16

Recalling Back

"Remembering before our God and Father your work of faith and labor of love and steadfastness of hope in our Lord Jesus Christ."
1 Th 1:3

The weather was freezing. This kind of season was tempting to just lay on the bed while hugging with your partner and sharing your own experiences of joys and sorrows. But for Mary Grace and Rencar Manteris, their relationship was as cold as the winter season. They see each other everyday, they eat together, they sleep together but they seemed to be far from each other as the stars in the sky; no more spark of sweetness between them. They just lived together. They seldom talked to each other even if they spoke everyday.

Their life revolved around a monotonous routine. Mary Grace usually wakes up ahead of Rencar to prepare their breakfast and helps her children to prepare for school. Then she prepares the coffee for her husband after he prepares himself for work. Rencar usually greets her wife with a kiss and then takes his breakfast and lives to work. Coming back from work, Rencar kisses her wife and puts down his bag, and turns on the Television. He would spend all his time before the T.V. He just turned it off when his wife would call him for dinner. On the other hand, Mary Grace usually stays at home. She gave up her work as a company manager just to take care of their three children. They lived a normal life as a couple. Their relatives and close friends looked at them as a perfect family. However, deep within them was a profound emptiness that endanger their relationship to end up abruptly. Both of them felt this way, but they just ignored it. They just went on with their life. Unfortunately, this empty space within them which results in coldness with each other was replaced by other pleasure. On one hand, Rencar spent more time drinking with his peers. On the other hand, Mary Grace was spending a lot of time in Sumba with her friends. As a consequence, they hired a helper in their house to prepare their food, who would do the laundry, would clean their house, and would watch over their children while they were out. They became used to this life; no time for each other and most especially no time for their children. They usually arrive home late when their children are already asleep. Even they enjoyed outside, but the emptiness was still there. What they were doing was all the more leading them to dig deeper into the abyss of nothingness.

One morning, during breakfast, Mary Grace and Rencar ate silently. They didn't talk for quite sometime already. The silence was so deafening. It was also irritating. And so Mary Grace broke the silence, "I think, we have a problem!"

He was shocked and looked confusedly at her.

"I'm serious! I think we should go for counseling," Mary Grace said.

"Why?" He was still confused. "I think; we don't have any problem?"

"I don't know!" She then stood up and went inside to their room.

Rencar knew she was angry. But he didn't know the reason.

On their bed, Rencar could not sleep thinking what his wife had told him. Mary Grace also was wide awake. She was thinking over the thing she had suggested to her husband. She didn't know why she said those things. She just wanted that their life would come back to normal where love and care were overwhelming. She recalled the enchanted memories they had when they were not yet married. They were so sweet and full of love. Their first five years as a married couple were amazing. Above all, they spent more time praying and hearing mass at the church. However, after six years of their marriage, they stopped hearing mass and seldom prayed together. Rencar also was recalling the beautiful memories he had with Mary Grace. He recalled the hardship he had undergone when he was still courting his wife. It took a year before Mary

Grace said yes to her love for him. He remembered also that Mary Grace used to bring him to hear mass when they were not yet married. Even though he was not used to going to church but because of Mary Grace's devotion to the mass, he was also learning to love the Eucharist.

He tapped the shoulder of his wife and said, "Do you want to hear mass tomorrow morning?"

Mary Grace turned his back to her husband and smiled, "Yes! It's a good idea."

"Okay!" He replied. "Good night."

"Good night, too."

They woke up at 5:00 a.m. They prepared themselves for the mass. They just lived their children to their nanny and went together. During the homily, the couple was carried away by the homily of the priest when he said, "As a couple when you already experience dryness and coldness with your relationship, it's better to go back with your love story where you are so in love with each other and recall how God blessed you with this love. Go back to that experience because it is only in recalling those lovely, enchanted, memorable, and precious moments which you will discover again the giftedness of each other which was given to you by God."

After the mass, they went home happy. They did their normal routine. But when Rencar arrived home from work, he invited Mary Grace for dinner outside without their children. Mary Grace was so happy. They talked the whole night, recalling their love story and celebrating the presence of each other, and thanking God for the gift of love that He had bestowed on their relationship as a couple.

They still do what they liked to do, but they prioritize the family affairs and one of those priorities is hearing mass regularly and praying together everyday.

Loving God, enkindle the love of all the couples who promised before the altar of marriage. Grant to them the grace to be always committed in their married life so as to grow in your love and faithfulness. Help them to become the example of your faithfulness towards humanity. We pray this through Christ who lives and reigns with You and the Holy Spirit, one God, forever and ever. Amen.

17

Signage

*"And the Lord's servant must not be quarrelsome
but kindly to everyone, an apt teacher, patient."*
2 Ti 2:24

Richard Bell must be there at his office at 8:00 a.m. As a manager of Stellar Communication Company, he has a regular meeting with his clients on Mondays. That was Monday and he got up late. It was already 7:00 a.m. His office was an hour away from his home. And so, he drove so fast to the office. When he was on the narrow road, he got stuck because the car ahead of him drove slowly. He overtook many times but failed. The road was too narrow. Cars on the other lane also lined up. He lost his temper. He blew the horn excessively. He only stopped when he saw signage at the back of the car he was following which says, "An 80-year old man is driving." His temper had slowed down. He grinned after reading it. He followed the car patiently until they reached the express highway. He overtook the car and saw the old man driving. He was smiling. He blew his horn as he smiled back at the old man. The old man did the same and waved his hands.

It was already 8:15 a.m. when he arrived at the office. He was fifteen minutes late from his regular meeting.

His secretary sat on her desk with a morose face. He greeted her, "Good morning, Mary."

She just opened her two lips to create a forced smile. But her face was sorrowful.

"Have the documents I needed already prepared?"

She handed the folders to him without a word.

"Thank you." He said.

She nodded.

"Is there any problem?" he asked.

She looked at him with her cloudy face.

Richard lost again his temper. He reprimanded her because of her disrespectful attitude towards him. He then went to his office. After a while, he came out for his meeting. Mila was still seated at her desk and sad; focused on what she was doing. He approached her to ask if the visitors were already at the conference room for their meeting. When he was near to her, he had seen that Mila was writing something on the paper. He read it, "I just broke up with my longtime boyfriend! It's so painful!" After she noticed that he was reading her note of brokenness on the sheet of paper, she tore it and threw it in the trash.

"They're waiting for you in the conference room, sir," she said.

"Okay!" he gently smiled.

He understood now why she acted that way. As a way of asking sorry, he patted the shoulder of Mary saying, "It's okay, Mary! Everything will be fine."

"Thank you, sir," Then she cried while recounting to him what had happened to her and her boyfriend. Richard listened attentively to her. After she unloaded her pains, she became relaxed and was relieved because someone listened to her. He also felt happy because he was able to help others in a simple manner.

It was already 11:45 a.m. when they finished their meeting. He was already hungry and it was already lunchtime. He lined up at the canteen for food together with his colleagues. The canteen was self-service. After getting his food, he looked for a table to eat at. The canteen was full. But fortunately, one table had a vacant seat. One lady occupied the other seat. She looked so stressed and problematic. He approached her and asked, "Can I sit here, ma'am?"

The lady did not answer him. She just moved a little so that he can put his plate on the table.

"Thank you, ma'am."

She said nothing. But five minutes later, the lady began scolding him because she just wanted to be alone and suddenly he arrived to share with her. She did not want a company. He listened to her complain and remained calm. He did not want to argue with the lady. But her litany of complaints against him continued so much so that he could no longer hold his patience and almost talked back to the lady. But when he was about to confront her and when he turned his face on her, he saw again the signage on his chest written, "I wanted to be alone, please! I just lost my mother." Reading it, his anger slowed down. And then he looked around to find another place to eat. On the other side, one table was already vacant. He got his plate and transferred there.

When he was already in his office, he reflected on what had happened to him. The three incidents which broke out his anger were telling him something. In his mind, he asked these questions, how about if I did not see or read their signage? I think there is a big possibility that I would release my anger to them indiscriminately. Do I need to see the signage of the problematic people in order for me to understand them and have patience with them, show my love to them anytime? But he was sure that all of those experiences taught him a lesson, be patient all the time and give them always the benefit of your doubt.

Loving God, teach us to be patient in every moment of our lives. Help us to show it in a manner that would lift up the spirit of others especially the dispirited one. Be our source of humility and kindness. Enkindle the fire of goodness within us so that we may show it to our brothers and sisters. Grant this through Christ who lives and reigns with You and the Holy Spirit, one God, forever and ever. Amen.

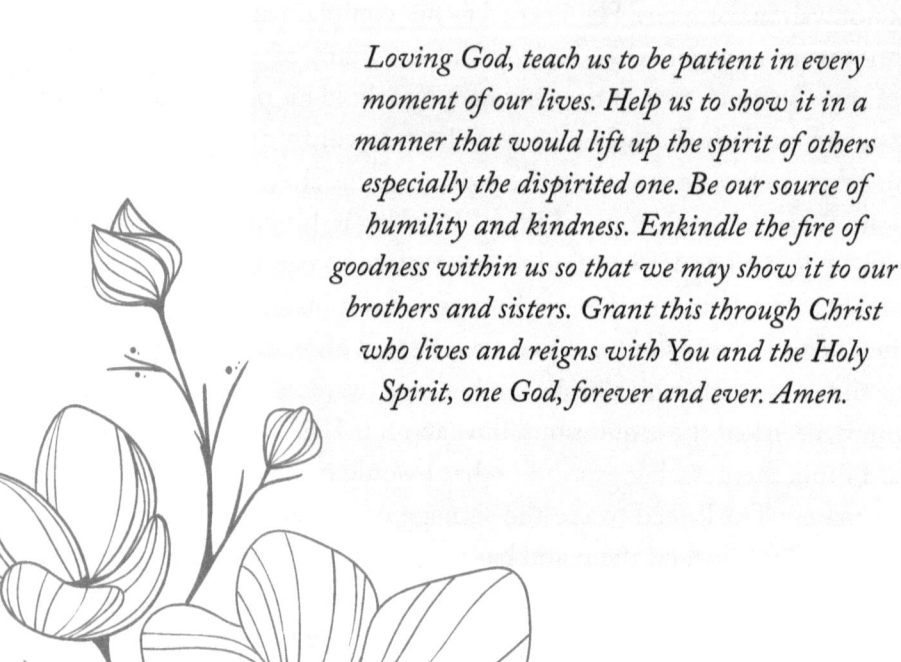

18

Simbang Gabi

"That is true. They were broken off because of their unbelief, but you
stand only through faith. So do not become proud, but stand in awe."
- Romans 11:20

Simbang Gabi, Dawn Mass, Misa de Gallo or Misa Aguinaldo have the same meaning for Filipinos. It is the most awaited time of the year aside of Christmas. People are excited to complete the nine days' novena mass in honor of Mary. The majority of the Filipinos believed that whoever complete the nine days of mass will surely receive their wishes. One of those who believed in this tradition was Randal Igpit. Since childhood, his mother had already inculcated in his mind the importance of completing the nine-day novena mass for the granting of all our wishes. Moreover, one important thing that was etched in his mind was the constant reminder of her mother, "Don't be late in the mass, your wish will not be granted."

"What time does the Simbang Gabi begin tomorrow?" Randal asked Nina, the secretary of the parish.

"4:00 a.m." Nina said.

"Thank you!"

"You're welcome!"

He bid goodbye to Nina and departed with his Red Mountain Bike. The travel time from his home to the parish is thirty minutes. He then prepared his dress for tomorrow's mass. He did not even take his dinner because of excitement. He went directly to his bed. Before sleeping, he thanked God for the blessings of the day. And he also offered a prayer that his wish will be granted; he prayed that God would give him the job that he was dreaming of, as an office clerk at Miralba Communication Center. He already sent his application letter. He was waiting for the interview. If his prayer will be granted, it will be his first job and a dream come true for him. This was his wish during the Simbang Gabi. He was determined to perfect the nine days' novena mass for that purpose.

On the first dawn of Simbang Gabi, he woke up so early. It was still three o'clock in the morning. He got up and prepared himself for the mass. He was wearing a red T-shirt, black pants, and a pair of blue sneakers. At 3:30 a.m, he was ready to go to the Church. He took his mountain bike and departed. Five minutes later, along the way, he saw someone lying on the road bathing with his own blood. He approached the man and asked, "What happened, sir?"

"Someone robbed me," the man replied.

"My God!" He said. "I'll bring you to the hospital!"

The man nodded. He hardly talked because he was already weak. Randal rushed him to the nearby hospital. It was already 4:00 a.m. when they arrived at the emergency room. The attending doctor immediately checked the patient. They did the necessary measure in order for the man to live. And they did well. The man was already saved. He was relieved after hearing from the doctor that the man was already stable. His T-shirt was full of blood. And then he remembered the Simbang Gabi. "Oh no! I have to change my T-Shirt. I'm already late!" He took his bike and went home to change his cloth.

When he was already near the Church, he heard the priest singing, "The Lord be with you!"

"And with your Spirit." The people respond.

"And may the Almighty God bless you, the Father, the Son, and the Holy Spirit."

"Amen."

"Go and announce the good news of the Lord!"

After the priest proclaimed the final blessing and sent of the people, Randal arrived. "My God! It's already finished!" He was so disappointed watching the people departing from the Church. He was sad thinking of his wish will no longer come true. He sat on the pew unloading his sadness to the Lord, "Sorry, Lord, I was not able to make it. You knew what happened." He then went out to the Church, got his Mountain Bike, and went home. The deep thought of missing the first mass of Simbang Gabi ruined his entire preparation to complete the nine-day novena mass. And of course, he was sadder because his wish will not be granted.

Early morning of the second day of Simbang Gabi, the cock crowed three times. Randal woke up on the second crowed of the rooster. He then removed the sleep crust on his eyes and checked the time. It was already 3:15 a.m. He got up from the bed and said a thanksgiving prayer to God while looking intently at the crucifix hanging on the wall of his room. After his prayer, he prepared himself for the mass. His body had fitted with his white polo-shirt and wore a black jeans. It was already 3:35 a.m. when he began traveling to the Church with his Mountain Bike. He arrived five minutes before the mass begins. The Church was already full. Some Church-goers arrived early in order to sit. So if you arrived late, you could not have the chance to sit, but stayed at the back and at the side of the Church. He stayed at the right side of the Church not so far from the sanctuary. Because of what happened to him the other day, his enthusiasm to complete the nine-day novena mass of Simbang Gabi had declined. The mass was going on, but his thoughts had traveled far away. His attention to the mass celebration was not 100%. He sighed oftentimes during the celebration. He kept on looking around the people, observing them, trying to interpret their facial expressions, "How many of them are present on the first day. They're fortunate because they have the chance to get what they are wishing for." Unfortunately, For the next two days, his thoughts were nailed thinking about all those things, and could not concentrate during the mass.

It was already the fifth day of the Simbang Gabi. Randall got up at 3:00 a.m., prepared himself, and went to the Church. However, along the way, one pregnant woman, with her five-year-old child, sat at the waiting shed. The boy was so worried looking at her mother who was struggling to breathe while holding her tummy. The mother was already weak. She could no longer speak.

He then stopped and asked the little boy, "What happen to your mother?"

"I don't know, sir," the boy replied while he was crying. "She just asked me to bring her to the hospital, and I don't know what to do."

"Where is your father?" Randall asked him.

"He is not here. He works abroad." he said. "Please help us. I don't know what to do. My grandmother just went home yesterday and she will probably come back this afternoon."

"Okay! Don't worry I will help you," he said. "Let me see, what we can do. Please wait here, I will call a motorcycle!"

"Thank you so much, sir, please be hurry, sir! My mother was already weak."

"Okay! I will," he said. "Please wait here a moment." He then went in haste to find a motorcycle.

The woman was already lying on the bench. Her child was rubbing her head and tummy.

"Ma! Please don't sleep," he said. "The motor will be here shortly! I already ask help."

The mother of the boy nodded.

Randall went to his neighbor, Renato, who was a motorcycle driver. He woke him up by knocking profoundly on his door's house and shouted, "Manong Renato, it's an emergency!" Of course, Renato and his wife suddenly woke up from the pounding of their door. They were so furious about the disturbance.

"Who is that?" Renato grunted. He got up and took his long bolo for protection if ever there was someone who would do harm to him. He slowly opened the door until it was open wide. He made sure that he had a good distance to defend himself from harm.

"It's Randall, manong Renato." he said. "I need your help. It's an emergency!"

"Is that you, Randall?" he asked this because his sight was still blurred because he just got up from bed. "Why are you here and why do you disturb us!"

"I'm sorry! I just need your help!"

"What help?" He said. "Is there any problem with your family?"

"No!" he replied. "One pregnant woman there in the waiting shed needs to be brought to the hospital immediately. She is already weak and lying on the bench."

"Really! My God! Let's go, now."

Renato got his motorcycle and both of them proceeded to the place where the pregnant woman was. When they arrived, the boy and the pregnant woman rode on the motorcycle and went to the hospital. They already arrived at the hospital at 4:00 a.m. The boy, Randall, and Renato were relieved when the pregnant woman was already in the delivery room. Thirty minutes later, finally, the grandmother of the boy arrived. That's why Renato and Randal had decided to leave them.

"What time is it," Randall asked Manong Renato.

"It's already 4:30 a.m.," Renato said. "Why?"

"I still have to go to mass."

"But it's already late."

"It's okay. Please bring me there!"

"Okay."

He arrived at the Church at 5:00 a.m. already. The mass had almost finished. The priest already prayed the post-communion prayer. So practically, he had still time to hear the announcement and received the final blessing. He again failed to hear mass completely. This made him so upset in for the next three days, although he was present in the mass, his desire for the celebration had slowly evanesced. He was present physically, but his mind had roamed around the Church looking at those faces of the people, commenting in himself how lucky those who can complete the nine-day novena mass.

Finally, it was already the ninth day of the Simbang Gabi. Randal got up so early and prepared himself. At 3:00 a.m., he was already inside of the Church. He sat on the front pew before the sanctuary. He looked around seeing again the faces of those people who came early for the last day of the Simbang Gabi. He gazed on the cross at the altar, observed the servers preparing the things for the mass, amazed with the lights on every corner of the Church. But suddenly, he heard the cock crows. When he opened his eyes, it was dark. He woke up and turned on the lampstand on the small table beside his bed. He groped to find the switch of the lampstand. When he found it, he switched it on. It was 2:30 a.m. He realized that he was only dreaming. He got up and decide to go early to the Church for the reason of thanking God for everything, for the blessings He showered upon him. The reason was no longer for his wish to be granted. 3: 15 a.m., he departed from the house and rode on his Mountain Bike. Fifteen minutes later, he saw one man with his flat tire car. So he approached him and said, "What can I help you, sir?"

"Good morning," the man replied. "As you can see, the tire is flat. Please help me fix it."

"Yes, sir! I can help you."

"Thank you so much."

"Where are you supposed to go?" the man asked him while he was removing the flat tire. "By the way, what is your name?"

"Randall Igpit, sir," he replied.

"I'm Vic Seriano."

"Nice meeting you, sir!"

"Me, too and thank you so much for helping me."

Randall smiled at him.

Fifteen minutes later, Randall had already changed the flat tire. "Okay, sir, it's already fixed," Randal said. "But bring it first to the shop, sir, to make sure that it's safe to drive."

"Okay! Thank you so much!" Victor thanked him. "By the way, here's my calling card, if you need some help."

"Thank you, sir."

"You are welcome. I have to go now. Bye."

When Randal looked on his wristwatch, it was already 4:30 a.m. He immediately got his bike and went in haste to the Church. The priest was already delivering his homily when he arrived. He stayed at the right side of the Church and prayed to God. He lifted up all his disappointments and asked God for his forgiveness.

Randall was so happy celebrating Christmas and New Year with his family. Because of this, he already moved on from his disappointments. But when he remembered that January 4 is his interview for the job he had applied for last time, he felt so nervous because it is his first time to be interviewed and he really longed for this job. And of course, he was nervous because the thought of not completing the nine-day novena mass had kept on bothering him and that he would surely fail in the interview.

January 4, at exactly 7:30 a.m., Randall was already at the office and waiting for his interview. There were also some people, like him, who were waiting to be interviewed.

When the secretary called him to enter, he began trembling. "You can enter now, sir."

"Thank you, ma'am."

When he entered the office, he saw one man sitting on the chair facing the back window of the office. He was talking to someone on the phone. Randall, while waiting, stood up for five minutes before the guy. When the interviewer, who happened to be the CEO of the company, turned his face towards him.

"Take your seat, please!"

Randall was taken aback when he saw the man, "Hello, sir! Good morning."

"Oh, Randal! It's you!" Victor said.

"Yeah! I don't know that you're the boss here."

"Yeah! I don't expect you to come here." Victor said. "Are you applying for the job or do you just want to visit me?"

"I came for the job, sir"

"Okay! No need the interview." Victor said. "You're hired."

"Sir!"

"I said, you're hired."

"Really!"

"Yeah! The person like you is the one we are looking for."

"Thank you so much, sir." He thanked Victor. "I'm so happy, sir."

"You deserve it, Randall," He said. "Welcome to my company." Then Victor shook hands with Randal, "Congratulations."

Sometimes we are carried away by the belief of most people which oftentimes leads us to forget the essential elements of our faith. Lord God reminds us always of this reality in times we tend to forget the essentials and inclined to trust the shallow belief of common people. Help us to transcend our faith in our daily devotion and charity. We pray this through Christ who lives and reigns with You and the Holy Spirit, one God, forever and ever. Amen.

19

Rosary

"On you I was cast from my birth,
and since my mother bore me you have been my God."
Psalms 22:10

"When you are tempted Fr. Joseph, pray the rosary and ask the help of our blessed mother," gentle reminder of Maria. She was the head catechist of San Roque Parish. She then handed the beautiful rosary she bought from Rome after their pilgrimage and indeed the Pope himself blessed it.

"Thank you so much, Nanay Maria," Fr. Joseph said. "I'll keep it as a precious gift."

"No! you have to use it," She said this like a mother who reprimands her child.

"Don't worry," he grinned. "I will pray the rosary every day."

Fr. Joseph Calvan was a newly ordained priest. He was assigned in San Roque Parish as an administrator. He stayed there for already a year.

Nanay Maria was worried about Fr. Joseph because she noticed that a beautiful, young and rich lady kept on visiting him in the convent for counseling. She trusted the integrity of Fr. Joseph, but she had doubts with that lady. She sensed something. As a way of helping him, she reminded him to pray the rosary daily. She believed that our blessed mother would always help us to overcome temptations by constantly praying the rosary.

After their conversation, Fr. Joseph departed to attend for their presbyterium.

After their meeting, he traveled back to the convent. It was already late. When he arrived, it was dark and peaceful. No people around. His cook, secretary, and the driver usually go home after their work. So no one stayed in the convent except for himself. In the parking lot, he saw a car. He then parked his car beside that car. He slowly opened the door and alighted while looking around the parking lot. He saw nothing. Walking on the path walk, before the convent he saw one man standing and was texting. He knew that the man was texting because of the reflection of the light from the cellphone. He could not recognize him. He tried to approach him with caution. When he was already near, he realized that she was a woman; the stranger wore a long dress with no sleeves. The cleavage was quite revealing. She had long shining hair and a perfect body. Her white complexion illumined the darkness of the night. Then the lady slowly approached him.

"Good evening, Fr. Joseph!" the lady greeted him.

"Good evening, Jeanie!" he was able to recognize her. She was the lady that Nanay Maria was talking about. "Do you have any matters here? Why are you here?" He saw that she was bringing pizza.

"I would just want to thank you Fr. Joseph for your advice," She replied. "It helps me to move forward in my life."

"Your welcome. I'm happy that I was able to help you," he smiled. "By the way, how many hours have you been waiting here?"

"Only an hour," she said while looking at her wristwatch. "It's okay. I just really want to see you."

"If you come here for counseling, let us better do it tomorrow if it's not really urgent because it's already late. Besides your husband and daughter are waiting for you now."

"I don't have a husband."

"Really! I thought you're already married because you said you have already a daughter."

"I am a single parent. But my child stayed at my mother's house. So I am free to do what I want to do. And no one will look for me now."

"Ah, I see. But you must go now because I need also to rest."

"Please! I just need a person to talk to and listen to my problems."

"Is it really urgent?"

"Yes! Because I want to end my life."

"Oh no! don't do it. Okay, let us talk. Just don't do it."

"Thank you, Fr. Joseph." She was already crying.

"Okay! Please wait for me on the balcony."

She nodded.

He changed his clothes in his room and followed her to the balcony. She sat on the couch beside the aquarium. Before the couch was a small table. On the table stood can beers.

"Why beers are here?"

She grinned.

"Are we supposed to speak? We will not do drinking sessions here."

"I know. I just want to speak with you casually, not like what we usually do in the counseling session. It's boring. Let us try to be spontaneous now."

"I can't drink with you in the convent. Please let's talk tomorrow."

She then began crying. "I would just want you to listen."

Because of her incessant crying, he gave in. They drank and had a conversation until both of them were already drunk. Jeanie began advancing towards him. And he also gave up on the temptation. They began doing indecent acts. They were almost there; Jeanie was already naked and so he was. He brought her to his room. When they were in the room, he accidentally hit the small table beside his bed and the rosary that Nanay Maria had given him dropped on the floor. When he saw it, he immediately recalled what Nanay Maria had told him. He then realized that he was already naked. He immediately left her and went in haste to Nanay Maria's residence and recounted all that had happened. He kept on crying to her while sharing everything.

"Our blessed mother really intervenes. Let us thank her for her protection," Nanay Maria said.

After that incident, he regularly prays the rosary. Temptations are always there but it helps him fight temptations.

Loving God, thank you for giving us a mother
that is so loving and caring for us who are weak.
She helps us overcome our temptations which
leads us always to sin. We ask you to bless us and
strengthen us through the intercession of our
Mother Mary to overcome the enticement of evil.
We lift up all this through Christ who lives and
reigns with You and the Holy Spirit, one God,
forever and ever. Amen.

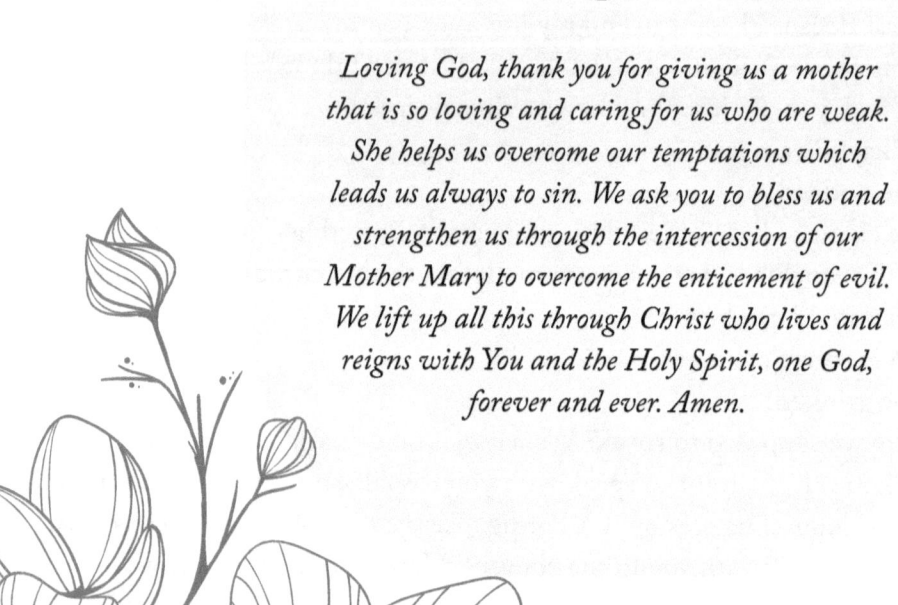

20

Writing Workshop

"Save me from the mouth of the lion!
From the horns of the wild oxen you have rescued me."
Psalms 22:21

The two men, wearing black helmets with their red 125 XRM Honda Motorcycle which had a carrier box at the back seat, stopped in front of Raymond Cervantes while he was grilling pork barbecue in front of their house. It was already 5:30 p.m. Riding in tandem was rampant in society today which was associated with crimes. Two persons have usually carried the crimes on the motorcycle. One would drive the motor and the other would execute the killing. There are ample reasons for the killing. He thought that the two men were riding in tandem who stopped to kill him. Out of fear, Raymond ran away fast inside their house. His mother, Elena, saw him running fast towards his room. She wondered and noticed that he was so afraid. She then went outside to know what happened there. When she was already outside, she saw a man standing just before their gate, looking inside their house. She asked him, "What can I do for you, sir?"

"Good afternoon, ma'am," the man greeted her. "Is Raymond Cervantes living here?"

"Yes! I'm his mother," she said. "Why are you looking for him?"

"I'm from the GVR delivery," he smiled. "Raymond has a letter from the UP Writing Club."

"Okay," she was confused about what the letter is all about. "Excuse me, I will just call him."

"Okay ma'am," he smiled again. "By the way ma'am, you can also receive the letter."

"Ah okay, I will receive it."

The man then handed the letter to her. She signed her signature on the receiving sheet which the man also gave to her. She handed back the sheet to the man. The man received it and went with his companion who just stayed on the motorcycle.

After the two men left, Elena went to Raymond's room and knocked on the door. Raymond did not respond. She entered and saw him at the window looking outside.

"What happened?" she curiously asked. "Why are you so afraid?"

"There is a riding in tandem outside, ma!" He was trembling while speaking.

"What are you saying?" she frowned.

"They want to kill me!"

"What?! She shouted. "Are you crazy! He's just a postman!" she hit his head with the letter whom the postman delivered.

"What is this?"

"I don't know what is that. He just said that it is from the UP Writing Club."

He immediately grabbed it and grinned. He opened it excitedly. When it was already opened, he exuberantly shouted, "Yes! I made it!"

Elena was so curious so much so that he grabbed the letter from him and read what was written there. "Wow! You made it! She grinned. "Congratulation my son!" She then hugged him.

"Thank you so much ma!"

"I'm very proud of you! It's a dream come true for you!"

"God is so generous ma," he cried on her shoulder. "He grants my prayer!"

"Yes, He is!" She confirmed what he said. "By the way, how's your pork barbecue?"

"Oh no! It is already burned," He scratched his head. "I left them outside!"

"There's no riding in tandem outside, okay?" she patted his back. "Finish grilling it so that we can sell it early."

The workshop will begin one week after he received the letter. The UP Writing Club shouldered all the expenses: round trip plane ticket, food, and accommodation. The organizer also required the participants to bring the necessary requirements for the workshop which are also attached in the letter. And so during that week, he spent his time gathering all his requirements.

Finally, a week later, he already gathered his requirements, and of course, his most awaited day had come. He woke up so early because of too much excitement. At 5:50 a.m., he was already prepared and was ready to go. His flight was at 10:15 a.m. with Cebu Pacific flight number Q8152018. He began traveling from home to the airport at 6:00 a.m. The estimated time travel from his home to the airport was two hours. He decided to travel early to avoid missing out on his flight. But there are events of our life that are so unpredictable. While he was humming his favorite love song, he saw from a distance a traffic jam. He was wondering why there was a traffic jam where indeed the road was so wide. And so he went out of the taxi and asked the driver before their car, "What happen, sir?"

"There's an accident!" the driver said.

"Really?!" He was disappointed. He reacted not because he was concerned with the victims of the accident but he was thinking of his flight. He went back to the taxi murmuring. It was already 8:15 a.m. They were already stuck up for thirty minutes and the situation became worse. He was already anxious which was manifested in his trembling knees and hands. He kept on watching on his wristwatch. There was already chaos; the drivers kept on blowing their horns and angrily shouted in the direction of the accident. They didn't hear any ambulance coming. The lack of immediate response of the rescue team had depicted the government's incompetence to address that particular incident. Raymond looked again at his wristwatch. It was already 8:30 a.m. and the airport was still an hour away. Missing his flight meant that his dream would remain in his wildest dream. Fortunately, at 8:45 a.m., they heard the siren of the ambulance. A light of hope had shined on his face. He then calmed himself when he saw the cars were already moving.

"Please move a little faster, kuya," he said. "I will be missing my flight."

"Yes, sir!" the driver said. Then the driver accelerated the speed of his taxi. His speed reached 90 kilometers per hour. They would probably arrive at the airport at 9:45 a.m. if the driver maintained the speed. As the taxi sped up, he fell asleep. But suddenly, the back tire of the taxi exploded. The driver struggled to control the steering wheel. Luckily, no vehicles had passed. The driver held tight the steering wheel so that they would not bump the trees beside the road until they reached the left side of the road and finally the taxi stopped.

"What happen, kuya?" he asked.

"The back tire exploded, sir!" the driver replied. He looked so pale.

"Oh my God!" He signed of the cross. "We are still fortunate that nothing bad happened to us."

"Yes, sir!" the driver said. "Thanks be to God."

When Raymond looked at his wristwatch, he was shocked, "Oh my God! It was already 9:30 a.m.! How much time do you need to fix the tire?"

"I think, I can fix it in thirty minutes!" the driver said.

"Really?!" he shouted. "I will be late if it takes thirty minutes to fix it."

"That's the faster I can do, sir. I'm very sorry."

He then decided to wait for a public bus and paid the driver. He was again trembling in anxiety. It was already 9: 55 a.m., but no public transport was passing. Fortunately, at 10:05 a.m., the driver already changed the back tire.

"Let's go, sir." He said. It's already fixed."

"Really?! Thank you so much, Lord." he praised God.

He rushed to the taxi and continued their travel. He was thinking that he could still catch up on the flight because they would surely give some allowance for those who were late.

But suddenly, after fifteen minutes of traveling, the tire of the taxi exploded again. Now it was the front tire that exploded. Hence, his world seemed to collapse. He became hopeless and had no chance for the driver to fix it because there was only one reserved tire. He should go to the vulcanizing shop to fix it but no shop was available in that place. He waited for public transport but there was none. At 11:05 a.m., the bus came and he rode.

He knew that he already missed his flight but he just went there in case the plane was still there. It was already 11:30 a.m. when they arrived at the airport.

He rushed to the information desk to ask if his plane was already flying. Sadly, the plane was already up flying ten minutes before his arrival. After hearing the bad news, he sat down on the bench of the pre-departure area, in front of a big T.V. screen, looking so hopeless. He raised his eyes to the big screen, then a flashed report caught his attention.

"Cebu Pacific flight number Q8152018 had just crushed. There is still no news about the survivors. Watch the whole story this evening in T.V Patrol," the reporter said.

Raymond checked the flight number of his plane, "Oh my God! That's my plane!"

Then his cellphone vibrated. He checked the message, "Dear Raymond, I am sorry to tell you that the schedule of our writing workshop will be moved next week. We already rebooked your ticket and we already sent it to your email. Thank you for your understanding." The sender was Tyron Bee, the communication officer of the UP Writing Club.

He cried and said, "Thank you so much, Lord God! You saved me and my dream."

Loving Father, you always extend your hands for us who believe in your divine assistance in times of troubles, calamities, accidents, and many other bad circumstances. Through this, help us always to trust you in everything and be confident in your saving works in the world. We lift up this through Christ who lives and reigns with You and the Holy Spirit, one God, forever and ever. Amen.

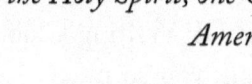

www.ingramcontent.com/pod-product-compliance
Lightning Source LLC
Chambersburg PA
CBHW052015170626
46808CB00007B/2948